In honor of
The Friends of the Neva Lomason
Memorial Library
September 2002

WE CAN READ!™

What About Bettie?

by Jacqueline Sweeney

photography by G. K. & Vikki Hart
photo illustration by Blind Mice Studio

BENCHMARK **B**OOKS

MARSHALL CAVENDISH
NEW YORK

For Kate Nunn and Dottie Griffin,
who care so much about Bettie

With special thanks to Daria Murphy, reading specialist
and principal of Scotchtown Elementary, Goshen, New York,
for reading this manuscript with care and for writing the
"We Can Read and Learn" activity guide.

Benchmark Books
Marshall Cavendish Corporation
99 White Plains Road
Tarrytown, New York 10591

Library of Congress Cataloging-in-Publication Data
Sweeney, Jacqueline.
What About Bettie? / Jacqueline Sweeney.
p.   cm. — (We can read!)
Summary: Mama helps Hildy wait as her brother and sister ducklings hatch
and to welcome Bettie, even though she is different.
ISBN 0-7614-1118-6
[1. Ducks—Fiction. 2. Animals—Fiction. 3. Brothers and Sisters—Fiction.]
I. Title II. Series: We can read! (Benchmark Books/Marshall Cavendish)
PZ7.S974255 Wf 1999   [E]—dc21   99-058289 CIP   AC

Printed in Italy

1 3 5 6 4 2

Characters

Hildy

Mama

Dee

Frankie

Bettie

Tim

Eddie

Jim

Molly

Gus

Ron

Mama Duck was sitting
on three eggs.
"I hear Dee," she said.
"Oh! There's Frankie.
There's Bettie!"

Hildy was watching.

"How can you tell?"

"By their sounds," said Mama.

"I know *each* one."

Hildy listened.

"I don't hear a thing!"

"You will," said Mama.

"When they hatch."

That night Hildy couldn't sleep.

Instead she listened—

to the crickets

to the wind

to the lapping of the pond.

Then she heard,
Tip Tip.

Was it coming from the nest?

Tip Tip Tip.

Hildy squawked, "Mama! Mama!
The eggs are making noise!"

"Dee is pipping," said Mama.
"She's pecking a hole
in her shell."

Tip Tip Tip

"Frankie's pipping too!"
"But what about Bettie?"
asked Hildy.

"Bettie's not ready," said Mama.

"Go back to sleep."

15

The next day Dee and Frankie
started to hatch.

"I can see their feet!" yelled Hildy.

Their shells began to crack.

Out plopped
two tired ducklings.

"They're wet," said Hildy.

Mama started flapping.

"Time to dry them," she said.

"Hildy, you flap too!"

"But what about Bettie?" asked Hildy.

"Keep flapping," said Mama.

Soon the babies were dry.

"They're fluffy," said Hildy.

"They're PEEPING!"

Then she made up a song:

Tiny black beaks
Tiny black feet
Pipping—Hatching
Peep! Peep! Peep!

At last Bettie started to pip.
She hatched by moonlight.

"She sparkles," said Hildy.
"But Mama—she's yellow!
And she has orange feet!"

Mama smiled,

"Your sister *is* yellow."

"With orange feet!" said Hildy.

"Bettie came to us,"
said Mama. "And I'm so glad
she's my baby."
"Mine too!" quacked Hildy.
"She's mine too!"

The next day the family
waddled to the pond.
The friends were waiting.

Mama quacked, "Meet Bettie,
Frankie, and Dee!"

"Hi, babies!" squeaked Molly.

"Hi, kids!" grunted Gus.

Eddie pointed.

"What about Bettie?" he asked.

"She's my sister," said Hildy.

"Hi, sister!" croaked Ron.

"Hi, sister!" squealed Tim and Jim.

Splish! Splish! Splish!

The new brother and sisters
took their first swim.

WE CAN READ AND LEARN

The following activities are designed to enhance literacy development. *What About Bettie?* can help children to build skills in vocabulary, phonics, and creative writing; to explore self-awareness; and to make connections between literature and other subject areas such as science and math.

BETTIE'S CHALLENGE WORDS

Discuss the meanings of these words and use them in sentences:

beak	brother	egg	flap
fluffy	hatch	listen	nest
noise	peck	quack	shell
sister	sound	squawk	

FUN WITH PHONICS

This activity reinforces blends. You can also adapt it for compound words, contractions, prefixes, and suffixes. Use white paper to cut out eggs about six inches long. Lay eggs sideways. Crack them by cutting zigzag lines across the eggs. (Cut each egg differently to create simple puzzle pieces.) On one half write the first part, or blend, for a word. On the other write the last part of the word. Have children match the halves to make a whole word and then read them out loud.

Blend words:

crickets	sleep	squawked	Frankie
grunted	friends	squeaked	splish
croaked	squealed	swim	brother

CREATIVE WRITING

A Listening Walk. Pipping, pecking, peeping, and cracking—so many sounds are used in Bettie's story! Enjoy the sounds in nature or in a big city. Take a listening walk. Bring along a clipboard, paper, and pencil.

Write down all the sounds you hear. Use these special words to write a "sound" poem. For example:

There was <u>pecking</u> and <u>pipping</u>
From an egg that was <u>tipping</u>.
It <u>peeped</u> and it <u>scratched</u>
With a <u>quack</u> it was <u>hatched</u>!

What About Bettie Was Special? Each character in the story has special qualities. So do each of us. Ask children to interview members of their family and write about their best qualities. Use paper precut to fit into small plastic sandwich bags. After children have written their descriptions, place each slip of paper in its own bag. Tape the bags together on both sides to create a miniature quilt celebrating the unique qualities within each child's family. You might illustrate your quilts by attaching drawings or photos of family members to the back of the papers.

POND ROCK THEATER

Children and adults can dramatize the excitement in Bettie's family. Draw pictures of the characters on white paper plates. Glue paint stirrers to each plate to use as handles. Reenact the story using the plates as masks. Create a new ending in case Bettie is still not ready!

READY FOR HATCHING

Learn about the life cycle of a chick or duckling through hands-on experience. A small incubator in a home or classroom brings the process to life. Local farms may provide fertile eggs. Help children research the hatching and growth of chicks and ducklings. They can record their observations on a daily basis until the day the eggs are ready. (Before you begin this project, be sure the farm will raise your chicks or ducklings.)

ARE YOU READY?

Bettie was not quite ready to hatch. Each person is ready to do things at different times. Children learn to walk, talk, and even read and write at different times. That's okay! Help children create a timeline from their birth date to the present. Make note of when children were ready to do things — crawl, eat solid food, catch a ball, ride a bike, have their first sleepover, and so on. Continue to add to this timeline whenever a special event occurs in their lives.

About the author

Jacqueline Sweeney is a poet and children's author. She has worked with children and teachers for over twenty-five years implementing writing workshops in schools throughout the United States. She specializes in motivating reluctant writers and shares her creative teaching methods in numerous professional books for teachers. She lives in Stone Ridge, New York.

About the photo illustrations

The photo illustrations are the collaborative effort of photographers G. K. and Vikki Hart and Blind Mice Studio. Following Mark Empey's sketched storyboard, G. K. and Vikki Hart photograph each animal and element individually. The images are then scanned and manipulated, pixel by pixel, by Mark and Kendra Empey at Blind Mice Studio.

Each charming illustration may contain from 15 to 30 individual photographs.

All the animals that appear in this book were handled with love. They have been returned to or adopted by loving homes.